For sax great Joshua Redman.
And to Lester "Pres" Young & Charlie "Bird" Parker
in sax heaven
—J.L.

To Becky, who bopped into my life and jazzed it up
—H.C.

Who Bop?
Text copyright © 2000 by Jonathan London
Illustrations copyright © 2000 by Henry Cole
Printed in the U.S.A. All rights reserved.
http://www.harperchildrens.com
Library of Congress Cataloging-in-Publication Data
London, Jonathan, 1947–
Who bop? / by Jonathan London ; pictures by Henry Cole.   p.   cm.
Summary: Hip hares and cool cats dance to the swinging music of Jazz-bo's saxophone.
ISBN 0-06-027917-6. — ISBN 0-06-027918-4 (lib. bdg.) I. Children's poetry,
American. [1. Jazz—Poetry./ 2. American poetry.] I. Cole, Henry, 1955–
ill.   II. Title.   PS3562.04874W48   000 98-26110 811'.54—DC21 CIP AC
Typography by Elynn Cohen
    2   3   4   5   6   7   8   9   10 ❖

Who Bop?

by Jonathan London • pictures by Henry Cole

HarperCollins*Publishers*

Who bop?
We bop.
We all bop
for be-bop!

Hip-hop
DOODLEE-WOP—
let's go
to the sock hop!

Jazz-Bo,
he's there
blowin' for
some HOPPIN' hares.

He plays sax with the cats
jammin' on stage.
Bobby socks
are all the rage.

A BING BANG DIDDLEE-WHAT,
put a scare in that snare!
Give it all you got—
then throw the sticks in the air!

Tickle the keys
and BOUNCE your knees.
Make black and white
light up the night.

Get down,
play that thing!
If it's got that swing
it means EVERYthing.

Jazz-Bo knows it.
Says, "Hope I don't blow it!"
He SQUEEZES them blues
right out of his shoes.

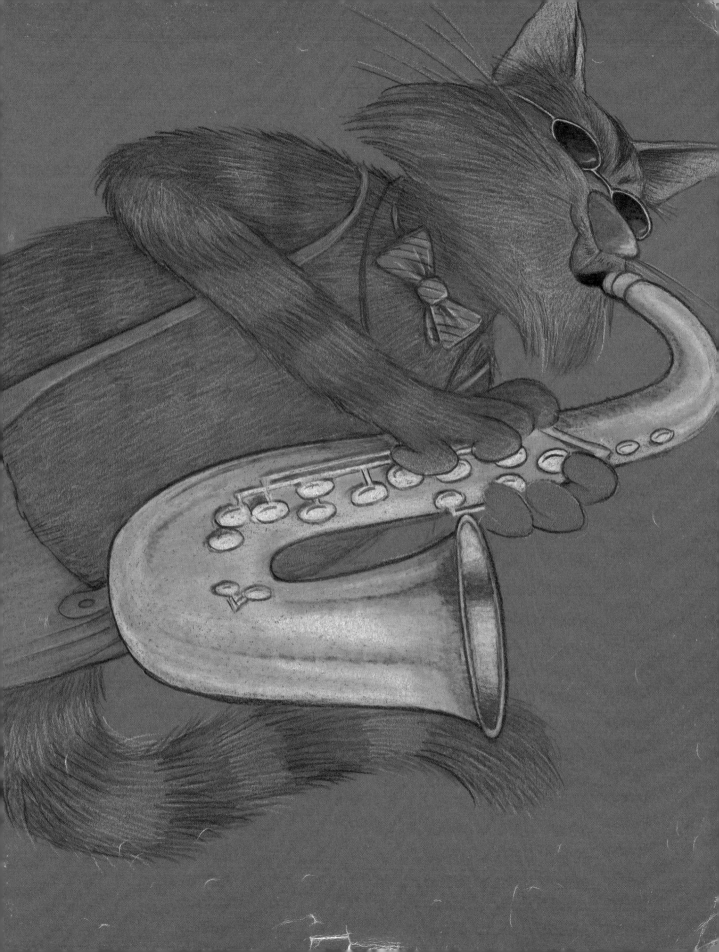

Jazz-Bo's sax
beats all the facts.
He makes his tunes
FLY like LOONS.

They swerve and they swoop
and they splash with a laugh.
They swim in a loop
and do a flip and a half.

Who bop?
We bop.
We all bop
for be-bop!
HIP HOP
DOODLEE-WOP—
let's go
to the sock hop!

The cats be blowin',
fingers flyin',
horns singin'
COOL as a lion.

So jump right in,
this is your chance
to SWIRL and SPIN
and DANCE DANCE DANCE.

TOSS that bunny,
SWING that girl,
dig it, honey,
give me a WHIRL.

Tap those toes,
SHAKE them hips,
snap them fingers,
and do some FLIPS!

We be HOPPIN'
to the sound
of the be-bop boppin'
goin' around.

HIP DE-DIP
and HOP HOP HOP,
we like to bo-bip
and do-wop the bop.

We be boppin',
hip-hop hoppin'.
There ain't no stoppin'
'til we be FLOPPIN'.

Who bop?
We bop.
We all bop
for be-bop!

Hip-hop
DOODLEE-
WOP—
let's go

to the sock hop!